The Nosemaker's Apprentice:

Chronicles of a Medieval Plastic Surgeon

by Nick Jones and
Rachel Shukert

A SAMUEL FRENCH ACTING EDITION

MUSIC USE NOTE

Licensees are solely responsible for obtaining formal written permission from copyright owners to use copyrighted music in the performance of this play and are strongly cautioned to do so. If no such permission is obtained by the licensee, then the licensee must use only original music that the licensee owns and controls. Licensees are solely responsible and liable for all music clearances and shall indemnify the copyright owners of the play and their licensing agent, Samuel French, Inc., against any costs, expenses, losses and liabilities arising from the use of music by licensees.

IMPORTANT BILLING AND CREDIT REQUIREMENTS

All producers of *THE NOSEMAKER'S APPRENTICE: CHRONICLES OF A MEDIEVAL PLASTIC SURGEON must* give credit to the Author of the Play in all programs distributed in connection with performances of the Play, and in all instances in which the title of the Play appears for the purposes of advertising, publicizing or otherwise exploiting the Play and/or a production. The name of the Author *must* appear on a separate line on which no other name appears, immediately following the title and *must* appear in size of type not less than fifty percent of the size of the title type.

In addition the following credit *must* be given in all programs and publicity information distributed in association with this piece:

**Originally produced by Terrible Baby Theater Company
in conjunction with the Brick Theater**

***THE NOSEMAKER'S APPRENTICE, CHRONICLES OF A MEDIEVAL PLAS-
TIC SURGEON*** was first produced by The Brick Theater & Terrible Baby
Theater Co. at the Brick Theater from May 1-May 23, 2009. The pro-
duction was directed by Peter James Cook, stage managed by Annalee
Fannan, with scenic designs by Aaron Gensler, costumes designed by
Normandy Raven Sherwood, lighting designed by Shaun Fillion, and
sound designed by Jo Williamson. The cast was as follows:

KENT/HARALD FLEETFOOT/HANS/

    ARNOLD-GUNTHER/RHONDA/PASCAL . . . . Rightor Doyle

GAVIN . . . . Eric Gilde

FATHER/NARRATOR . . . . Ian Lowe

WULFRIC/ULRICH/JEAN-MICHEL/QUEEN . . . . .Corey Sullivan

GIRL/AMELIA . . . . Molly Ward

CHARACTERS

(for 4 males, 1 female)

FATHER/NARRATOR

LITTLE GIRL

GAVIN

WULFRIC – an English Nosemaker

ULRICH – a Viennese Nosemaker

KENT – the Gatekeeper

SIR PERCIVAL – a mutilated knight

AMELIA – daughter of Wulfric

PASCAL – a French Manservant

The **QUEEN** of France

JEAN-MICHELLE – Director of the Free Clinic in Paris

WAITER at Café Gruel

FEMALE RECEPTIONIST

HAROLD FLEETFOOT – a messenger

ARNOLD-GUNTHER

HANS – the Wife Smeller

(*A* **LITTLE GIRL***'s bedroom. Darkness.* **FATHER** *and* **LITTLE GIRL** *enter.*)

LITTLE GIRL. See? I cleaned my room.

FATHER. Very good, Julie, very good. Now let me your see your teeth.

(*She shows them.*)

Good…You flossed too?

LITTLE GIRL. Yes.

FATHER. And applied moisturizer?

(*She makes a face.*)

Julie, you need to apply moisturizer every day to protect your skin.

LITTLE GIRL. Daddy, I'm eight.

FATHER. I know. But unprotected exposure to the sun can cause premature aging. You saw what happened to your mother.

LITTLE GIRL. Is that why you stopped loving her?

FATHER. No, of course not. And I never stopped loving her, I just got sick of looking at her, and listening to her nag.

LITTLE GIRL. She just wanted you to get a job.

FATHER. I have a job. I'm a plastic surgeon.

LITTLE GIRL. Mommy says you're not a real plastic surgeon unless you have a license.

FATHER. Yes, well, Mommy thinks she's very smart. But if Mommy is so smart, then why is she so poor? And why does she have to make you share a room with her and Jim when at my house you have your own room?

LITTLE GIRL. That's true.

FATHER. Well, goodnight honey.

(He kisses her and turns to leave.)

LITTLE GIRL. Wait! Daddy?

FATHER. Yes, sweetheart?

LITTLE GIRL. Am I pretty?

FATHER. Of course you are, sweetheart. Why do you ask?

LITTLE GIRL. I don't know. I just thought, if you *didn't* think I was pretty, you could always give me some free plastic surgery…I know you said I needed to wait until I was eleven, but I thought maybe just…a little tummy tuck.

FATHER. Honey, I can't.

LITTLE GIRL. But why not?

FATHER. Because. People won't understand. I could make you look like the most beautiful woman in the world…

LITTLE GIRL. Joan Rivers?

FATHER. Right. But the other kids at school would notice you had had work done. They would be jealous, and they would make fun of you.

LITTLE GIRL. But why?

FATHER. Because some people – people like your mother – are stupid. They don't approve of people trying to look and feel their best, even as they obsess about it themselves in secret. That's why there are doctors like me, who can make people beautiful under the table, at an affordable price.

LITTLE GIRL. Mommy says plastic surgeons aren't necessary. She says they're a modern blight.

FATHER. There's nothing modern about wanting to be beautiful, honey. Nosemakers have been around for thousands of years.

LITTLE GIRL. Nosemakers?

FATHER. That's what plastic surgeons used to be called: nosemakers. For when the knights lost their noses in battle to dragons, or proud ladies lost them to disease, they required nosemakers to fashion new noses out of wood.

LITTLE GIRL. Wood? Who'd want a nose made out of wood?

FATHER. You would, if you had no nose at all. A nose of wood, or tin, or papier-mâché…Back in the middle ages, they didn't have the science we have today.

LITTLE GIRL. Right.

FATHER. There were great noses, too. Noses commissioned by lords and kings, made of gold and encrusted with emeralds and rubies. And there is a legend, of a nosemaker who once forged a nose made of real human flesh…What I wouldn't give to have seen that. They say you could hold it in your hand and see its nostrils flare…as if by magic. Come here.

LITTLE GIRL. I'm already here.

FATHER. Good. Because I think it's time I told you a long story…

LITTLE GIRL. But I have school tomorrow.

FATHER. …The story of the Nosemaker's Apprentice.

(Music begins.)

In England, in the olden days, people lived short brutish lives, but they were short brutish lives full of magic and wonder. It was a time when kings walked the earth, when wizards were actually taken seriously; and lo, t'was the golden age of Nosemaking. The art was young and crude then. So disfigured was most of the population in those days that almost anything could be considered an improvement. Nosemakers were in demand. And so it happened one stormy night, that an old nosemaker named Wulfric didst one day knock upon the iron gate of the Ivanhoe Workhouse for Criminally Impoverished Boys, to seek an apprentice for his noble craft.

(Wind howling. Huge ominous knocks on a door that are loud and threatening.)

GATEKEEPER. Who goes there?

WULFRIC. It is Wulfric, son of Arathorn.

GATEKEEPER. Wulfric, son of Arathorn, from whence have ye come?

WULFRIC. From the hamlet of Ogilvy-on-Mather. I am Nosemaker there.

GATEKEEPER. Nosemaker, eh? Then prove it.

WULFRIC. Excuse me?

GATEKEEPER. Fix my nose, and ye shall pass. Fail, and ye shall know my steel.

WULFRIC. Good gatekeeper, how am I to assist thee, if I cannot see your face? Throw open the gate and I shall dispose upon you the greatest of my art.

GATEKEEPER. Smart guy, eh? You think I'm stupid, smart guy? You think I'm just going to let you in here for nothing? How do I even know you are who you say you are? How do I know you're not a bandit or a highway-man?

WULFRIC. *(wearily)* Very well. Describe to me your ailment, and I shall tell you what to do.

GATEKEEPER. Okay. Well we had this boy here, see, Angus? Blind boy, everyone felt sorry for him at first, until he became surly. Not his fault of course. At night some of the bigger, more retarded boys had been amusing themselves by dropping things in little Angus' empty eye sockets. Lit matches, mouse turds –

WULFRIC. So it was this boy who somehow damaged your nose?

GATEKEEPER. Oh no, no. I could have heard him coming from a mile away, on account of the shackles all the boys wear. No, it happened one night when I was sitting up drinking with Ethelbert the Fat, the morning gatekeeper. Ethelbert bet me a talon of silver I wouldn't take my knife and cut off my own nostril. Well, I wasn't going to let Ethelbert call me coward. So I took my knife and cut my nostril clean off. Figured I'd just go to the barber once I'd sobered up and have him sew it back on.

WULFRIC. And your country barber-surgeon botched the job, no doubt?

GATEKEEPER. No! He never even got a chance. Angus ate it! Poor little devil probably figured it was a scrap of ham. But the point is, now I'm walking around with a lopsided proboscis like a damn fool.

WULFRIC. I see. Well, my friend, I believe I can tell you how to repair your mangled protruberance.

GATEKEEPER. Saints be praised!

WULFRIC. Gather a bit of the dried spleen of a badger, the bile from the bladder of an ox, and a scoop of the honey of a bee.

GATEKEEPER. Okay.

WULFRIC. You have all those things?

GATEKEEPER. Yup. I got 'em right here.

WULFRIC. Good. Now fashion a curl cut from the spleen. Take the bile and the honey and mix them with the tip of a pure silver knife until they form a thick paste. Then with the knife, make two clean cuts across your palm in the shape of the Holy Cross of the Christian Christ. Then dip the curl of spleen into the mixture and affix it to your face.

(There are a variety of squelchy sound FX as this is done.)

GATEKEEPER. It's a miracle! I look even handsomer than before!

WULFRIC. I have done as you asked. Now honor your promise and throw open this gate!

(Sound FX: door swinging open)

GATEKEEPER. Wulfric, son of Arathorn, Nosemaker of Ogilvy-on-Mather, I am your servant!

WULFRIC. Thank you…

GATEKEEPER. Kent.

WULFRIC. Kent of…

GATEKEEPER. Of nothing. Just Kent.

WULFRIC. Very well, just Kent. I have come this day to buy a boy.

GATEKEEPER. Of course, of course, for you anything. Come, I'll take you to the north tower, where we keep the blonds.

WULFRIC. No, Kent, I do not seek this boy for pleasure, but for work. Every day, more and more knights return from the battles of the Holy Crusades, missing noses, ears, and other small appendages...

GATEKEEPER. God bless.

WULFRIC. We honor their service. But alas, the good Lord has blessed me with more orders than I can possibly fill. And so I seek from among the unfortunate youths here at Ivanhoe an apprentice. A likely lad, to whom I may pass down the ancient secrets of nosemaking, and treat as if he were my own dear son.

GATEKEEPER. Well! I think we can help you out there. Just follow me.

(The sound of footsteps down a long hallway. They walk for a very long time, in awkward silence.)

So, did you see the joust the other day or...

WULFRIC. No.

(More steps.)

GATEKEEPER. Boy, this is a long corridor.

WULFRIC. Yes.

(More steps. Finally –)

GATEKEEPER. Here we are! I'd hide any rings or other valuables. And make sure your beard and penis are tucked safely inside your clothes. Some of these little bastards get grabby.

(Sound FX: unlocking, and door swinging open. Terrible ruckus – screaming, chaos.)

Hello Roger, you're looking fine today. No new sores I can see. Oh no, there's one; I thought that was one of your eyes. But Liam, you look well! Liam here is a good strong lad. That's why we keep him in all these chains.

WULFRIC. Good! I need a strong boy to hold down my patients when I operate on them. But this boy looks insane. What else have ye?

GATEKEEPER. If you wanted someone not insane, why didn't you say so? In the strong but not insane department, we have Godfrey here. You've heard of the Minotaur? Very strong, half bull half man? That was his father. He left Godfrey here in a basket. You can see the resemblance to a cow. He looks like a cow, doesn't he? Doesn't he look like a cow?

WULFRIC. That is because he is eating the grass growing from between the floor tiles. Because he too is insane.

GATEKEEPER. Oh, is that it?

WULFRIC. Kent, I require a boy who is strong and smart, as well as sane. I know you must have such a boy, and I know you are probably just trying to offload some of your more desperate cases on me first.

GATEKEEPER. What? What are you talking about?

WULFRIC. As much as I would like to take all these wayward children into my home, I have room for but one, and he must be fit. Now, show me the good stuff.

GATEKEEPER. You are shrewd, Nosemaker. Very well. Let's go in the back.

(Sound of a giant door opening, followed by another door, portcullis, drawbridge crank and what-have-you.)

Gavin, come on out boy.

FATHER. From out of his cell came the golden haired youth. His bright blue eyes, shining within dark circles, were kind, intelligent and sane looking. The boy's face was smeared with soot and flecked with rat bites; and though he was thin from his meager workhouse diet, the lack of fat reserves displayed a natural musculature, which truthfully, was kind of amazing.

WULFRIC. What is your name, boy?

GAVIN. Gavin, sir.

WULFRIC. Gavin. My name is Wulfric. And from whence cometh you, and from what location?

GAVIN. I know not from whence I come sir, nor from which location, for I have spent my entire life here at Ivanhoe.

GATEKEEPER. We keep him away from the other boys because we feel there's something special about him. He is born for some great work. Perhaps someday he may even become a Gatekeeper, like me.

GAVIN. Kent, you flatter me. I am not smart or brave enough to be a gatekeeper – they are the hardest jobs to get!

WULFRIC. Now boy, let me see your hands…Yes, they are strong. They are nosemaker's hands. But how are your reflexes?

GAVIN. Good, sir. Throw a rock at me, and you'll see.

WULFRIC. No need. I can tell your mind is – HHUAAAH!!

(He throws a rock at him, which **GAVIN** *dodges.)*

Kent! Huzzah! This is the boy I've come for!

GAVIN. Come for? Are you to take me away, sir?

GATEKEEPER. No Gavin, don't worry, you're not going any-where…

WULFRIC. But he may!

GATEKEEPER. No! No, it's not possible. He's my favorite. I can't give him away. I should never have shown him to you.

WULFRIC. But I am offering the boy a grand opportunity. You would not keep him here, just for your own amusement?

GATEKEEPER. You've seen the other boys. Who else am I to going to talk to? But look, I'll tell you what: I'll let you have him if you take me, too.

WULFRIC. Kent…

GATEKEEPER. No, really! Then you'll get two apprentices for the price of one. I mean, I don't want to be here any more than he does!

GAVIN. But Kent, I love it here. Why would I want to leave the workhouse where it is safe and I am loved?

GATEKEEPER. I don't know! But he's trying to take you away, and if you go, I want to go too!

WULFRIC. Kent, I cannot take you!

GAVIN. Then I don't want to go either.

WULFRIC. But Gavin, my boy, there is a whole world outside that you have yet to discover. You will come to work with me in my shop, and I will teach you many things. I will teach you how the world is balanced on the shell of a giant turtle, and how wind is created by the giant wings of celestial eagles.

GATEKEEPER. Well, sounds like you've already told him, so…

WULFRIC. Outside there is a world more beautiful than any you have yet imagined. Where I live in town, you will have your own bed, and from your window you can see my grove of English Pines every morning.

GAVIN. Does it smell there sir? Like here? Like human feces, all the time?

WULFRIC. No, it smells like lavender and honeysuckle, merely balanced with notes of human feces. But a likely lad shouldn't mind a bit of stink, if he has his freedom.

GATEKEEPER. You are right. It is so. You do not belong here, Gavin.

GAVIN. Kent? Do you mean it?

GATEKEEPER. Yes. Go with the Nosemaker. He will teach about noses, and giant eagles, and sunsets. Things you cannot learn here. So go, but only promise me you will return from time to time…

GAVIN. Of course I will return to you, Kent. How could I live without occasionally visiting you and all the wonderful staff at Ivanhoe?

FATHER. And so they left the Ivanhoe Workhouse for Criminally Impoverished Boys, Gavin's old home to which he would never, ever, ever return. In the bare sunlight for the first time, Gavin winced as if blinded, and batted his hands in the air.

GAVIN. Oh my god! What is that thing??

WULFRIC. That, my boy, is called the sun.

FATHER. It was the most terrifying thing he had ever seen – though of course, he was still young. Gavin pleaded for Wulfric to release him, but the old nosemaker held his arms firmly, guiding him forward through this frightening new world of daylight. The old nosemaker's hands were strong, but his voice was kind, and by the time they came to his cottage in town, Gavin already felt that he trusted him.

(They approach a cottage, with a sign that reads: Wulfric Nosemaking and Repair: Inquire Within.)

WULFRIC. Come in, come in. Don't be shy. This is now your home too, after all.

GAVIN. Yes sir…it's just… *(His voice breaks.)*

WULFRIC. Saints preserve us! Is that a tear I see? Is it a wee tenderhearted pixie I have chosen for my heir?

GAVIN. I'm sorry sir. I'm overwhelmed. No one has shown me such kindness since my own dear mother, and she died long before I was born.

WULFRIC. And your father?

GAVIN. My father is dead too. He died before he even met my mother.

WULFRIC. Poor lad. Orphaned before you were even conceived.

GAVIN. Yes, sir.

WULFRIC. I'm sorry if I was harsh with you just now. But you must learn to contain your emotions. The art of making false noses, ears, and other small appendages is an exacting science, and often a gruesome one at that. You must discipline your mind and your body. For you never know what horrors may be revealed to you when the masks be lifted and bandages unfurled.

GAVIN. Whatever do you mean, Master Wulfric?

WULFRIC. All in good time, my boy, all in good time. You are looking rather peaked. I expect you'll be wanting your tea. Amelia!

FATHER. And all of sudden, young Gavin thought he would fall to his knees. Not with weakness, but with prayer. For now entered the room the most beautiful girl he had ever seen. Her hair was like spun gold, her eyes like emeralds. Her figure was graceful, her cheeks pink as seashells. But most beautiful of all was her nose. It was perfect. It was the most beautiful nose Gavin had ever seen. 30 degree angle off the face. Straight bridge, not too big, not too nostril-y…

AMELIA. Yes, Father?

WULFRIC. Ah, there you are. May I present my daughter, Amelia. Amelia, this is Gavin. He'll be living with us from now on.

GAVIN. Hello.

AMELIA. Hello.

WULFRIC. There! Now that we've introduced you, why don't you go and make us some tea? Bring the meat bones too, with plenty of gristle. This is a celebration. Now be quick!

AMELIA. Yes, Father.

(There is a heavy knock at the door.)

MESSENGER. Master Wulfric! Open the door! It is I, Harald Fleetfoot, with an urgent message!

*(**HAROLD** enters.)*

WULFRIC. Harald! Wonderful to see you! It looks like that otter snout is setting in nicely. Won't you join us for some tea?

MESSENGER. Would that I could, but I can't! The knights have returned, from the Holy Land! Their ships have docked at Penhaligon this fortnight past, and now they beat a path to your door! You must prepare yourself Master Wulfric. They will be arriving any minute.

WULFRIC. And are they horribly disfigured?

MESSENGER. Aye. Some you would hardly know for men, were it not for the helmets and armor and shit. And they have done things most foul to themselves in the interim. I saw a knight with the trunk of an elephant, and another wearing a Saracen's face over his face. Many are blind, and all of them are crazy.

(Sound FX: commotion-screams of agony, cries and lam-entations and anger.)

Here they come now! Stay, I dare not. Harald Fleetfoot, out!

*(Sound FX: wind whooshing as **HARALD** runs away.)*

WULFRIC. Yes, I see them! There beyond the brae! Huzzah, children, we haven't much time. Amelia, fetch the bandages and the smelting tools. Gavin, prepare the soldering iron and distill the laudanum. And don't forget to bring me the blood of a slut and collect the semen from the griffin in the backyard! Quickly!

GAVIN. But –

AMELIA. Don't worry. I'll help you.

WULFRIC. Huzzah! Huzzah! Huzzah!

(Commotion gets louder and more frantic as the disfig-ured knights descend on the nosemaker's cottage.)

KNIGHT. *(offstage)* Nosemaker! Nosemaker!

WULFRIC. *(exiting to meet him at the door)* Ah hello, sir. Lost it again have we? Well don't worry, we'll fix you right up…

GAVIN. Collect semen from a griffin?

AMELIA. Not semen, just boiling water.

GAVIN. But how do I get it out of the griffin?

AMELIA. No, silly, he just wants us to get him some boiling water! It's a code.

GAVIN. So, you don't have a griffin?

AMELIA. I wish! No, my father gives all his instructions in code, so that any eavesdroppers will not learn his secrets. He forgets that you are new! But I will teach you. Collect semen from a griffin just means boil some water. If he wants you to really collect semen from a griffin, he'll say "take out the trash."

GAVIN. And what's the blood of a slut?

AMELIA. It means he needs a cup of coffee. It's going to be a long night.

FATHER. And so it was. The knights came in an endless procession, demanding remedies for their various ailments. The first knight suffered from a horrible gash in the septum. But with a sprinkling of lead powder and peat moss in the wound, Wulfric stitched it right up. The next knight was missing an ear and eye as well as a nose, from a single scimitar slash from horseback. He was on his way home to his family and was afraid his children would not recognize him. Wulfric fashioned him a new nose out of wood, gave him a smooth painted pebble for an eye, and sewed on the ear of a horse to replace the missing one. He went away happy and eager to surprise his children. More knights crowded into the shop, each one a unique case. Wulfric treated them all with kindness as he shouted his cryptic instructions to Gavin, which Amelia then translated. Although by the end of the night, she hardly needed to…

GAVIN. Here is your Hair of Saturn, Master Wulfric, and another cup of Slut's Blood – two Ball Sacks and extra Fire of a Racoon's Belly, like you like it. Oh but Master Wulfric, where did all the customers go…?

WULFRIC. I have sent them away, till the morn. My eyes are failing. I can work no longer…

AMELIA. Yes, Father, you must rest.

WULFRIC. I could not have done my work tonight without you, Gavin. You have proved most useful.

GAVIN. Thank you, Master Wulfric. I am honored to help. Your work helps so many people live semi-normal lives. Tell me, where did you learn this great art?

WULFRIC. Ah, I had a mentor. His name was Ulrich, from Austria. There, there are great schools, where they teach the very latest in pseudo-science and magic. He taught me the basics. Alas, I had not the funds to complete my studies, so the rest I have learned myself, futzing around. England is not a learned place. There are few practitioners as I. It makes my duty all the more important.

AMELIA. And tiring. Come father, you must to bed.

(A mighty knock at the door.)

WULFRIC. I am closed for the day, sir! Come back tomorrow.

(Another knock is heard.)

Much as I would love to see it, friend, I must retire now. I will see you in the morning.

(Another knock, accompanied by a low growl.)

I know it is morning technically. I mean come after I have had time to rest.

PERCIVAL.   BRAAAHAHAHHAHAHAHHHHHHH HHHHHHHHHH!!!!!!

(Sound of door being knocked in, and a blasting wind outside.)

FATHER. Before them stood a dark and bloody hole, oozing pus and bile, like the gaping maw of Underworld itself. Master Wulfric cried out in terror.

WULFRIC. *(brandishing his staff/cross)* Devil begone! Ye shall not take me yet!

(sounds of a struggle)

Gavin! Amelia! Run from this place!

AMELIA. No Papa! I won't leave you!

WULFRIC. Foolish girl! Your father is damned! Save yourselves, I beg of you!

AMELIA. No!

GAVIN. Master Wulfric! This is no devil! It is a man!

WULFRIC. What ho?

FATHER. And the Nosemaker forgot his fear, for he saw that the boy was right; that the hole before him was the ruined, mangled face of Sir Percival, his landlord.

WULFRIC. Milord! Forgive me! I did not recognize you!

SIR PERCIVAL. BRAAAAHHHHHH.

WULFRIC. Please, milord. I bid you enter.

SIR PERCIVAL. BRAAAHHHHHHH.

WULFRIC. No, Milord, I beg of you. Don't cancel my lease. Please, allow me to examine that I may at once assess your gruesome situation.

SIR PERCIVAL. BRAAHHHHHHHHH!!!

WULFRIC. Of course, of course. My daughter Amelia shall make you comfortable.

SIR PERCIVAL. BRAAAAHHHHHHH!!!!

WULFRIC. Naked? You…wish…to disrobe, Milord? I don't have a problem with that, if that's what you –

SIR PERCIVAL. BRAAAAHHHHHHHH!!!!!

WULFRIC. Oh, you mean Amelia should get naked, yes of course. Allow me to avail you of my arts, and then you can do whatever you want to my daughter.

AMELIA. Father!

WULFRIC. Hush, child! Sir Percival is our landlord. If we should displease him, he will throw us on the streets, and then we'll all have to be prostitutes anyway!

AMELIA. But it's not fair!

WULFRIC. Well, Missy, if you think you're too good for the feudal system, you can just invent some other organizing principle of government. In the meantime, go harvest a kidney from the Loch Ness monster and marinate it in the saliva of an encyclopedia salesman. Go!

*(**AMELIA** and **GAVIN** run off to do these things.)*

GAVIN. Amelia, I don't understand. How can your father ask such things of you?

AMELIA. Sir Percival is a powerful man. He owns all of the village and most of the shire, and is a specialmost friend to the King himself. Should my father run afoul of him...oh! It is too terrible to imagine.

GAVIN. Try.

AMELIA. I cannot, I cannot. But let me say this...my father didst displease Sir Percival once.

GAVIN. How?

AMELIA. Twas on my parents' wedding night. Sir Percival was but a boy, no more than eight years old, but he arrived that night with all his men, ordering my mother to submit to his rights as lord. My mother was proud. She refused him. And my father refused to force her.

GAVIN. And?

AMELIA. And, in the night, while my father slept, Sir Percival returned with all his eight and nine year-old henchmen and stole my mother away. In the morning, my father found her tied to a tree. Her throat was slit. She was dead. My mother was dead before I was even born.

GAVIN. Mine too!

(*Romantic music swells as they have a moment.*)

Amelia?

AMELIA. (*quickly*) Yes?

GAVIN. If I was your father, or even your...husband, I'd never make you have sex with anyone you didn't want to.

AMELIA. Oh, Gavin. Don't say such things.

GAVIN. I mean it.

AMELIA. If that were true...I...

GAVIN. It is true. Oh, Amelia. You're the most beautiful and only woman I've ever seen. Your skin is like the moon, and you have the most perfect nose. 30 degree angle off the face. Not too big, not too nostril-y...

AMELIA. Yes. It was my mother's. It was the thing about her my father loved most.

GAVIN. Amelia, I am only a poor orphan from the Ivanhoe Home for Criminally Impoverished Boys. I can't give you money or social standing, or even a ring made out of metal. So I'm going to tie these blades of grass around our fingers, and then we'll be engaged. Okay?

AMELIA. Okay.

FATHER. And so the Nosemaker's Apprentice and his Amelia were betrothed. But before they could seal their contract with a kiss, there was a terrible cry.

SIR PERCIVAL. BRAAAAHHHHHHHHHHHHHHHHHHH HHHHH!!!!!!!!!!!!!!!!!!!!!!!!

WULFRIC. Sir Percival, forgive me. Your wounds are beyond my art. Mercy, mercy, mighty one!

*(***PERCIVAL*** roars. Scene returns to* **FATHER** *and* **LITTLE GIRL**.*)*

FATHER. BRAAHHHHHHHHHHHH!!!!! He said. BRAAHHH HHHH!!! BRAAAAAHHHHHHH!!!!!!!!

LITTLE GIRL. But what –

FATHER. BRAAAAHHHHHHHHHHHHHHHHHHH!!!!!!!!!

LITTLE GIRL. But why couldn't he fix him, Daddy? Why couldn't Wulfric fix him?

FATHER. Why couldn't he? Or why *wouldn't he?*

LITTLE GIRL. You mean, he could have?

FATHER. He could have, if he weren't bound by the draconian rules and strictures of the Medieval Nosemaking Association. Even back then, there was all kinds of bullshit.

LITTLE GIRL. You mean, ethics?

FATHER. Yes. Wulfric could not operate on Sir Percival because he recognized his injury as one that was a result of his own sin. He had contracted a very severe case of syphilis. Do you know what syphilis is?

LITTLE GIRL. Of course! It's a kind of cooties that makes you blind and insane. Sometimes it makes your nose fall off. You get it from whores.

FATHER. That's right! And in the old days, you could tell a syphilis victim from how it ravaged their face. If a Nosemaker were to help such a case as Sir Percival then he would be disguising his disease, and likely people would agree to do…grown up things with him, like fucking him, and then they would contract syphilis. And then he could have been sued, and might even lose his license.

LITTLE GIRL. But who cares about a license? If Sir Percival was their landlord…and could kill them.

FATHER. I know honey. It seems insane. But Wulfric, for all his skill, was a simple man – like your mother – and had bound himself to the hypocritical repressive strictures of the Nosemaker's Association over what was good for his family.

(returning to the story)

Wulfric, Gavin, and Amelia did not sleep well the next few weeks, fearful that Sir Percival would seek revenge. But, the faceless knight did not return. No eight and nine year-old henchmen came to do to Amelia as they had done to her mother. And so the village came to believe that Sir Percival had died of his injuries or moved far away, and all seemed well again. The weeks turned to years, and the Nosemaker became quite prosperous, renowned for his skill, as well as for his dashing young apprentice. For long gone was the pale hairless boy that Wulfric had first seen at Ivanhoe. Now, well fed and properly exercised, Gavin had turned into quite a male specimen, with bulging biceps, a hard stomach and well-defined rear haunches…The fashionable ladies of the town began to submit to minor operations just so they might exchange a few words with the town stud.

*(**GAVIN** enters, now bigger and more muscular.)*

AMELIA. Gavin, was that Mistress Purdy the Washerwoman I saw you talking to?

GAVIN. Yes. Back for a graft of duck fat for yet another chin. These women just never feel plump enough. It's not their fault; it's the painters, creating impossible ideals of beauty. Regular people don't have food enough to get that fat. They can barely afford minor surgery!

AMELIA. *(muttering)* Maybe if she had less surgery she could afford more food.

GAVIN. What?

AMELIA. I think she fancies you.

GAVIN. Oh Amelia, don't worry, you know I have given my heart to you. Do I not still wear the blade of grass on my finger? Oh, where did it go?

AMELIA. You lost it!

GAVIN. I forgot! I took a bath last year!

AMELIA. You do not love me!

GAVIN. I do!

AMELIA. Then when will you marry me?

GAVIN. Soon, Amelia. When I am a licensed nosemaker with mine own shop, so I can take care of you properly and we can make the beast with two backs without your father listening. I believe I have already mastered all I need to know.

WULFRIC. *(entering)* Oh Gavin, that's true. Methinks you're the greatest nosemaker in all the realm…

(terribly)

PSYCH!!

GAVIN. Master Wulfric, excuse my impudence! I only meant, I believe my skills are adequate for the licensing exam, not that they exceed your own.

WULFRIC. Your skills are great, my apprentice. But your soul still has much to learn. You should never have grafted that duck fat onto Mistress Purdy.

GAVIN. But I only wanted to help her look and feel her best.

WULFRIC. There are lepers in the street who have lost their fingers and toes and penises. That duck fat would have been better used on them. A nosemaker's work is not to improve upon the work of God…

GAVIN & WULFRIC. …but to mend it when ravaged by the Devil.

GAVIN. Forgive me, Master Nosemaker. I am still unclear about the distinctions between reconstructive and cosmetic surgery.

WULFRIC. You must understand that the human soul is manifested through the face. If we tinker too much, we risk changing its very nature. And then I could lose my license!

AMELIA. And what, father, of a man who has no face? What can we say about his soul?

FATHER. The memory of Sir Percival sent a chill up their spines, one by one.

(A chill passes up their spines, one by one.)

WULFRIC. You do good work, Gavin. But operating on a woman is not the same thing as operating on a man. On a woman you can make small mistakes and convince her they were on purpose, but a man will brook no such nonsense

*(Suddenly, **WULFRIC** throws a rock at **GAVIN**. **GAVIN** ducks, expertly.)*

Just testing your reflexes…Gavin, I have something I want to give you.

*(From a hiding place, he draws out a package and hands it to **GAVIN**.)*

Open it.

GAVIN. *(He opens the package.)* Wulfric, it's your old crucible!

WULFRIC. It's a Travel Crucible. It belonged to my father, Arathorn of Lubriderm. He was an amateur alchemist of great talent, and it was his hope that I would follow in his footsteps. Alas, I had no talent for the Magical Sciences. But you, my boy, you possess the Gift. My father would be honored to know that it is yours now…were he not dead.

GAVIN. Wufric, I'm overwhelmed, I can't tell you how much this means to me.

WULFRIC. Look inside.

(**GAVIN** *lifts the lid of the crucible and finds a giant wad of cash.*)

GAVIN. What is this?

WULFRIC. Money, Gavin. I have saved it to send you to the Nosemaker's Academy in Vienna.

AMELIA. Father!

WULFRIC. You have seen how I reattach animal noses to my patients to replace their lost human ones. This is not strictly orthodox. There are other newer, more legal techniques, and you must learn them, if you are to become a great nosemaker.

GAVIN. But master, this is enough money to build a castle…

WULFRIC. College is fucking expensive, that's no joke! But you are worth it, my boy. I love you like a son. Go to Vienna and return a great nosemaker, that I may love you like a son-*in-law.*

AMELIA. But how long must he go for?

WULFRIC. The degree program is a minimum of 6 years.

AMELIA. What? No! We cannot be apart for so long!

WULFRIC. Of course, it depends where he does his residency…

AMELIA. I could not bear it! I must go with him!

GAVIN. Oh Amelia, surely many couples before us have weathered a long distance relationship. Besides, I'm sure I'll be too busy studying to even think about fooling around with any other girls. Don't worry. I trust myself.

FATHER. And so, with an ostensibly heavy heart, did Gavin bid a fond farewell to Master Wulfric and his fair Amelia and set off on the sailing ship that would ferry him to the legendary Nosemaker's Academy in the magical land of Vienna.

(proud Vienna music)

Vienna! Pride of Austria! Center of the Known World! A seat of learning, home to great medical minds like Sigismund of the Orient and Gottfried, Lord of the Clean Hands. To legendary alchemists like Albrecht the Paranoid, Balthazar the Nude, and Ambrosius the Bisexual. And of course, the most famous and brilliant of them all, Johann Amadeus Ulrich, Supreme Nosemaker of the Universe, Headmaster of the Royal Nosemaker's Academy, whose office Gavin now entered.

(jingle or sound of door opening)

GAVIN. Hello?

RECEPTIONIST. Ja, come in.

GAVIN. Is this Admissions?

RECEPTIONIST. This is the office of Dr. Ulrich. Admissions are closed. Our term began four months ago.

GAVIN. But it took me four months just to get here from England.

RECEPTIONIST. An Englishman, ja? Typical. Well, I'm sorry but the term is closed. You'll have to wait till next year.

GAVIN. What? But you can't turn me away. Please, just let me speak to someone.

RECEPTIONIST. You're already speaking to someone. You're speaking to me. And I told you no.

GAVIN. I thought this was a fraternity of Nosemakers! I thought you cared!

RECEPTIONIST. I'm sorry. I'm just the Receptionist. I don't get paid enough to care.

ULRICH. But I do!

GAVIN. Doctor Ulrich! Is it you?

ULRICH. Do not worry, young Gavin. We will find a place for you.

RECEPTIONIST. But Herr Doktor! This *Lesbearschgesicht* is four months late!

ULRICH. Europe needs Nosemakers! It is our duty to train them. Besides, he's English and we're trying to increase our racial diversity.

GAVIN. Thank you, Herr Doctor, thank you!

ULRICH. It is nothing. It is my belief the Nosemaker's Academy of Vienna should be open to everyone…

(Triumphant music begins. Secretary stands up excitedly.)

Except women!

(She sits back down.)

Welcome, young Gavin. Welcome to the Nosemaker's Academy of Vienna!

FATHER. And then they started to party. Because Gavin had arrived just in time for the weekend, and there's no college campus that parties harder than the Nosemaking Academy of Vienna on the weekend. Down went the books and out came the flagons of ale. Boys were shouting, they were taking their shirts off, and everybody was just fucking partying their asses off!

LITTLE GIRL. *(offstage)* Daddy?

FATHER. It was awesome!

LITTLE GIRL. Wait, daddy. Are you sure you're not projecting your own college experience onto the story?

FATHER. Oh well, maybe I am. I'm sorry. I just get so excited when I remember medical school. Ah, Brazil…

LITTLE GIRL. I feel like the Nosemaking Academy of Vienna would be more serious.

FATHER. You're right. The boys never took their shirts off. It was too cold, and it was very serious. It was at the Academy that Gavin learned standardized methods of nosemaking. His very first class was taught by none other than Doctor Ulrich himself.

(ULRICH lays out surgical tools on a table, while HANS, a nose-less volunteer subject waits on the operating table.)

ULRICH. Gentlemen! In our previous lessons, we have seen how ears can be mended using bits of fabric, how chins can be extended to preposterous lengths, and how boils can be sewn together to form ornaments in the shape of snowmen. These were merely academic exercises. Today we focus attention on the nose itself! The nose! The seat of the face! Where a man's soul finds its most articulate expression. Today we are fortunate to have a volunteer subject. Everyone say hello to Hans!

(Class says hello.)

HANS. *(in noseless nasal voice)* Hello.

ULRICH. Hans as you can see has lost his nose. It was cut off for smelling another man's wife. Well, Hans, did you actually do it?

HANS. Of course I did! And I'll do it again!

ULRICH. Very good. I will now attempt, without anesthetic, to sew a wooden nose on the patient's face.

HANS. Uh oh.

ULRICH. Hans, are you ready?

HANS. Yeah! Do it!

ULRICH. Then I will manacle you to the operating table…

GAVIN. Excuse me, Doctor Ulrich.

ULRICH. Yes, Gavin? What is it?

GAVIN. Would it not make a finer prosthesis if the nose were fashioned of some organic material, such as seal bladder or alligator gums?

(A wave of disdainful snickering runs through the room.)

ULRICH. You cannot make noses from animal parts.

GAVIN. But you…can.

(awkward silence)

ULRICH. Perhaps you can in England, but in Vienna you *may* not! It is an affront to God to mix the tissue of man with the tissue of beasts. To do so has been decreed a violation by the church and the Nosemakers' Association.

GAVIN. Then, what about a nose made from human flesh?

ULRICH. It is impossible. Even Ambrosius the Bisexual couldn't do it, what makes you think you can? Now if that is all, then let's begin…

GAVIN. But Doctor Ulrich…perhaps the right Nosemaker has simply not come along?

ULRICH. This is not a seminar, Gavin, it's a demonstration. Now kindly be quiet!

(Scene changes to **GAVIN** *walking away after class. He is upset.* **ARNOLD-GUNTHER** *approaches.)*

ARNOLD-GUNTHER. Hey, Tommy Englander, wait up! I'm Arnold-Gunther. I liked what you said back there, about making noses out of animal parts.

GAVIN. You did?

ARNOLD-GUNTHER. Yeah. It was comical.

GAVIN. It wasn't meant to be comical. I don't understand. Don't people in Austria want false noses that are soft and supple? Isn't that preferable to a cold, unfeeling nose of metal or wood?

ARNOLD-GUNTHER. It's all politics, man. The Academy has to watch itself, you know, with the Church. They question what we do. They say it smacks of witchcraft.

GAVIN. The church is one thing, but God is another. I think we have a responsibility to do whatever it takes to help people…

ARNOLD-GUNTHER. Yeah, I totally agree. But hey listen, we are all going to the tavern in the square to get wasted and pay some homeless people to let us operate on them. You in?

GAVIN. Oh, I don't know. I've barely unpacked. And I just got a letter from my girfriend…

(taking out the letter)

ARNOLD-GUNTHER. A letter, huh?

*(He grabs it from **GAVIN**.)*

GAVIN. Hey give that back!

ARNOLD-GUNTHER. Look, I'm Gavin. I have an English girl-friend with big boobies and a high voice.

GAVIN. No she doesn't!…

ARNOLD-GUNTHER. She doesn't…?

GAVIN. I mean she does, of course she does, they're huge, but that's none of your business, now give that back…

ARNOLD-GUNTHER. *(He begins reading in a high voice.)* My dearest darling Gavin –

*(**AMELIA** appears.)*

AMELIA. I miss you so much. It seems like ages since I have seen you. So much has happened since you left us to seek your fortune at the great Nosemaking Academy in Vienna. Father has been ill of late, and as he sold all our earthly goods to pay for your schooling, I have begun to take in washing to cover our expenses.

ARNOLD-GUNTHER. Oh, this is personal. Here you can have this back…

GAVIN. No, please keep reading. You sound just like her.

ARNOLD-GUNTHER. Okay…

AMELIA. Never fear. When my mind turns to unpleasant things, I imagine it is you who will eat the concoction of beaks and nettles I am sterilizing for our supper. When I am called to apply poultices and unguents to the afflicted, I imagine it is your oozing sores, your scrofulous genitalia that I am tenderly bathing, and my heart bursts forth in golden song. Study well, my angel, and hurry home so we can finally be wed!
All my love and more,
Your…

ARNOLD-GUNTHER. *(in girl voice)* Amelia.

FATHER. Gavin decided writing to Amelia could wait. Making friends was important and so was getting hands on experience. Among the campus at large, Gavin became known as Steady Hand Englander for his skill with the scalpel. Arnold-Gunther and the other students took to making bets on how many shots of tequila it would take before Gavin wavered in an incision. It took plenty. Gavin was one of those special students who could drink harder than anyone, partier harder than anyone, and still pull off a gentlemen's C. One day he was called into the office of Doctor Ulrich.

*(**GAVIN** enters holding a beer.)*

GAVIN. Doctor Ulrich, you wished to see me?

ULRICH. Yes Gavin, come in. I have called on you because I need your assistance. I have been asked to perform an emergency facial overhaul on the Duchess of Gervais.

(He throws off a sheet, revealing the Duchess on a gurney.)

She is to be married in several weeks time to the Prince of Borania, delivered as a virgin bride…but as you can see, she is not pretty.

GAVIN. Doctor Ulrich, this woman has contracted syphilis.

ULRICH. So what about it?

GAVIN. We cannot operate on her. It is unethical. A Nosemaker's job is only to restore that damage done by the Devil, not that which is self-inflicted. This woman has defiled herself and gets the punishment she deserves.

ULRICH. Impudent scamp! Who are you to say what she deserves? The syphilis of the duchess is congenital.

GAVIN. I don't know what that means.

ULRICH. It means she is a virgin. She has committed no sin.

GAVIN. Master Ulrich forgive me, I was just following the Code. Master Wulfric always told me that if you don't follow the Code you could lose your license…

ULRICH. Forget about getting your license. You think this is about you? You are a nosemaker. You are a servant of God. Your duty is to help people. The Code was only made to minimize the damage people like Wulfric can do…

GAVIN. But Wulfric is…

ULRICH. Wulfric is a two-bit hack! But you are different kind of hack, Gavin. It kills me to see your talent wasted.

GAVIN. I'm not wasted. Who's wasted?

ULRICH. Gavin come here.

GAVIN. I'm already here.

ULRICH. Good. Have you ever heard of a place called France?

GAVIN. Where the naked ladies dance?

ULRICH. That is only a legend. I have just this week received a letter from the free clinic of Paris. They have been overwhelmed with a plague epidemic and are desperate for nosemakers.

GAVIN. But Master Ulrich, it's only my fourth year of study!

ULRICH. You have great surgical skill Gavin, but you are arrogant and naïve, and you have a drinking problem. At the free clinic you will gain experience. You will learn patience and humility. But beware. For Satan is everywhere in France, and you are an at-risk student.

GAVIN. Master Ulrich, please! I'm not ready to leave college!

ULRICH. That's what Wulfric said, too. But I have no room for super-seniors. I know you have made many friends in Vienna, and there are some teachers who like you. But when it comes down to it, the best teacher you will ever know is right here, in your hands.

GAVIN. Is he invisible?

ULRICH. Listen to your hands. That is how you learn. Do not listen to your clients. Do not listen to your colleagues. Do not even listen to me, except for just now, when I said listen to your hands. Now get out of my office.

(Scene changes to **ARNOLD-GUNTHER** *and* **GAVIN** *saying goodbye.)*

ARNOLD-GUNTHER. Man, I can't believe you're going. I'm going to miss you, like, a lot.

GAVIN. Don't worry, Arnold-Gunther, I'll stay in touch. If college has taught me anything, it's how to have a long distance relationship. I haven't seen my girlfriend Amelia in years…

ARNOLD-GUNTHER. I know. Did you ever get around to writing her back?

GAVIN. I haven't had the time. But that doesn't mean we're not still together. That's my point. Love transcends words and actions and feelings.

FATHER. Gavin thought about writing Amelia to tell her that he was leaving Vienna and to give her his new address in Paris, but he decided it would just make her worry. She might have heard about the place with the naked ladies too.

DAUGHTER. So wait, Gavin got expelled?

FATHER. Technically, it was leave of absence. The official reason was because he was drinking too much, but everyone knew the truth. Gavin was asked to leave because he was so beyond the troglodytes at the Nosemaker's Academy of Brazil!

DAUGHTER. Vienna!

FATHER. Right, right. So anyway, Gavin stole a horse and drove to Paris. He arrived two days later – dirty, tired, cranky, just like a real Parisian.. And so began the darkest period of Gavin's life.

GAVIN. Bonjour! Are you Jean-Michel, the clinic director?

JEAN-MICHEL. Oui.

*(***GAVIN** *hands him the letter.)*

Eh, what is theez?

GAVIN. A letter of recommendation, from the Nosemaker's Academy of Vienna.

JEAN-MICHEL. You don't have a license?

GAVIN. Is that a problem?

JEAN-MICHELLE. Non. The lepers will not know the difference.

*(Shows him to an examining room, where a Frenchman, **PASCAL**, is waiting in a chair.)*

This will be your examining room. We have only the most basic tools, but you will find some tree branches and scrap metal for prosthetics.

GAVIN. It smells like urine.

JEAN-MICHELLE. It should. We use it for disinfectant. So whenever you need to go pee, try to pee on something that looks dirty. Here is your first patient.

GAVIN. Sir, I just arrived on horseback. I require rest and succor. Besides, I can't speak French.

JEAN-MICHELLE. Well, I don't have time to teach you. I am in the middle of bleeding a man and I don't want him to die before he gives me his insurance number.

(exits)

GAVIN. *(to **PASCAL**)* Hello there. What can I do for you?

*(**PASCAL** gives a long explanation, in French, speaking in a calm manner, like one would address a hairdresser.)*

GAVIN. Yes, I see your nose is a bit big. Perhaps if I cut it down a little?

PASCAL. Oui.

GAVIN. Or perhaps it's your weak chin that needs more definition?

PASCAL. Oui. Oui.

FATHER. Ulrich's voice came to him from far away.

ULRICH. Do not listen to your clients, do not listen to your colleagues, do not even listen to me, except for just a moment ago, when I said listen to your hands.

GAVIN. Okay. Here we go!

FATHER. It turned out the patient was just looking for a haircut. But after he stopped screaming, he was very pleased with the work Gavin had performed, and so was Jean-Michel. That night, he took Gavin out for gruel at a well-known gruel place, called the Café Gruel.

(Lights up on Café Gruel, a well-known Gruel Place. Ambient restaurant noises, piano music.)

WAITER. Welcome to Café Gruel. Our specials tonight are the Gruel a l'orange, Gruel avec les chanterelle mushrooms et les very small peas, and Gruel dauphinoise. We also have a gruel-encrusted halibut on a bed of braised gruel, and a very nice duck breast, which we call a duck breast, but is actually a mound of gruel.

JEAN-MICHEL. Shall I order for you?

GAVIN. Oh, yes, please.

JEAN-MICHEL. Very well. For me, I will have the gruel filet, cooked very rare, And for my companion, the entrecote de gruel, with a side of gruel.

WAITER. Very good, Monsieur.

(The **WAITER** *exits.)*

GAVIN. This place is really nice. Very…romantic. I hope you don't think…

JEAN-MICHEL. Don't worry, Gavin. I have no plans to seduce you. It was never my intention to intoxicate you and take you back to my hut, where we might eat leftover gruel from each other's bodies by the light of a candle made from human fat. No. That is the last thing on my mind. *(pause)* I have brought you to this dimly lit restaurant for another reason.

GAVIN. What is it?

JEAN-MICHEL. Gavin, I want you to take over as director of the free clinic.

GAVIN. What?

JEAN-MICHEL. Work at the clinic is difficult for me. I am… how do you say…a delicate flower. But today, I see you. Your hands are so soft as you do the work, like the hands of a butcher who makes sure the horse feels no pain. I said to myself, Jean-Michel, your work is done. God at last has answered my prayers. The chosen one has come.

GAVIN. But Jean-Michel, I have no qualifications, I –

JEAN-MICHEL. I can't take it anymore!! The screams, the smells, the unending poverty! If you do not take over, I will lose my mind! And my soul!

WAITER. Monsieur?

JEAN-MICHEL. WHAT?

WAITER. There's an errand boy outside with a message for you. He says it's urgent.

JEAN-MICHEL. Of course. *(to GAVIN)* Excuse me. *(He exits.)* Oh yes, I almost forgot…this letter arrived for you just yesterday…

GAVIN. It's a letter from Amelia…I never wrote her about my transfer…how the hell did she find me?

(opens the letter, begins to read out loud as AMELIA overlaps)

GAVIN/AMELIA. My dearest darling Gavin –

AMELIA. It has been three days since my last letter. For this slight I am deeply sorry, and I hope you will find it in your heart to forgive me. As referenced to you in my letter of June the 15th, our situation has continued to deteriorate. On the days when Father manages to rouse himself from his pallet, he puts on a brave face, but I believe even he has grasped at last the utter hopelessness of our circumstances… *(She continues, sotto voce, as WAITER interrupts.)*

WAITER. Can I get you anything to drink?

AMELIA. Oh, Jesus Christ. *(exits)*

GAVIN. Oh no.

WAITER. What's the matter? He's buying.

GAVIN. Oh, it's not that, it's just –

WAITER. AA? I gotcha. Listen, you should stop by the meeting down on Napoleon Street, that's where all the cute guys go. And here's my number, if you ever need to talk or…anything.

(fanfare of trumpets)

Oh shit! It's the Queen! It's the fucking Queen of France! Get down!

(another trumpet fanfare)

FATHER. All made way as the Queen of France stalked through the Café Gruel. Little cupids fluttered their wings in front of her, scattering rose petals made out of diamonds along the floor.

(WAITER *and* GAVIN *bow.*)

QUEEN. Who is this handsome boy? Speak!

GAVIN. Your…your majesty, they call me Gavin. I am a Nosemaker, newly arrived from Vienna.

QUEEN. Nosemaker! *(to* WAITER*)* What broad shoulders he has. Tres *masculin.* Tell me, Nosemaker, are you dining alone?

GAVIN. Uh, no…I was actually having dinner with my boss, Jean-Michel.

QUEEN. The director of the free clinic? Oh, but my dear boy, I regret to inform you that Jean-Michel is dead.

GAVIN. What?

QUEEN. Yes. He committed suicide in the parking lot just now, with a piece of piano wire held by one of my footmen.

GAVIN. Well, then I guess I'm having dinner with you.

QUEEN. You are impudent. I love this. Waiter! A bottle of your finest fermented gruel. At once!

(WAITER *runs off.*)

GAVIN. That's very kind of you, your Majesty, but I'm trying not to drink –

QUEEN. I don't care about your problems. Now, tell me the truth. Do you think I am beautiful?

GAVIN. Of course! Your Majesty is the most beautiful woman in the world!

QUEEN. You flatter me, but you are wrong! It is true, I am the most beautiful woman in France. But I am not the most beautiful woman in the world. My spies tell me that currently, the most beautiful woman in the world is a Slovakian countess named Brankovicza the Wonderful. This makes me very sad. *(She pouts.)* It is my intention to overtake Brankovicza the Wonderful as the most beautiful woman in the world at the Annual Most Beautiful Pageant in Baden-Baden this year. For this, I require a Nosemaker's help. And they say you are the best.

Now. As you can regard, Nosemaker, I am very, very, very, very fat. I am the fattest woman in all of Western Europe.

GAVIN. But your Majesty, your tremendous girth is what makes you most desirable.

QUEEN. Last year! Last year it was desirable! But this year the fashions have changed! Brankaviscza the Wonderful is slim, like a peasant. The new woman must be very *actif*, very *sportif.* You must slice open my body and suck the fat from me like a glutton sucks the marrow from a bone. I wish to have buns of steel and thighs like two green beans.

GAVIN. But your Majesty, much as I would love to help you, I have come here to work in the Free Clinic, for the Glory of God…

QUEEN. I am a noble, and related to God. My Glory should be good enough. In my palace you will be able to practice your art without interference. You will have many better tools than the Free Clinic, which is anyways being burned to the ground as we speak…I will treat you well, Gavin. Do not worry about a thing.

FATHER. Gavin went to live in the Palace of the French Queen. This was the fabulous town-palace where the Queen lived when she was in the city. Gavin was dazzled by the Queen's rare urns and giant tapestries. He found the Queen a kindred spirit at first…

GAVIN. I love your urns!

QUEEN. I am glad you like my palace, Gavin. And I am pleased with the job you have done on me. I feel one hundred pounds lighter.

GAVIN. Indeed you are, your majesty.

QUEEN. The only thing I am not quite pleased with is the massive scarring. Is there not anything you can do for that?

GAVIN. It is quite beyond my art to accelerate nature's healing process, your Majesty. But if you keep your clothes on, I don't think anyone will notice.

QUEEN. Ah, but that is not possible. I am French, and we… do this thing. But please, rest now. Tomorrow we will do the rest of the work.

GAVIN. The…rest?

QUEEN. But of course. You did not think this was all? I want big boobs, like a Spanish Lady. And full lips, like an Italian. And big eyes, like a big bug.

GAVIN. Your Majesty, you are already so beautiful, if you ask my opinion…

QUEEN. And you are sweet, both in looks and taste. But it is my taste that counts here, and I do not yet feel like my outer self matches the innermost beautiful self that is inside me, that is who I truly am.

GAVIN. But your Majesty, there are no known procedures for what you ask of me.

QUEEN. You will find them! After all, you are the greatest and most sensual Nosemaker who has ever lived! And of course, you must conduct experiments. Pascal!

(PASCAL, *the patient from the clinic appears.*)

GAVIN. It's you! From the clinic!

QUEEN. Pascal will manserve you, and you may experiment on his body.

PASCAL. Bonjour.

QUEEN. And now I shall retire for the evening. You may join me, once you have finished your work.

FATHER. There was little choice to be made. Gavin took a long quaff of the very good Scottish whiskey that Pascal had brought him on an engraved silver tray and let his hands do the rest. The next morning, the Queen came to see what he had come up with.

GAVIN. Your Majesty, I have worked tirelessly through the night, but I believe I have at last come upon a solution. Allow me to introduce you to your new breasts. Pascal!

(**PASCAL** *enters. He now had enormous breasts, which make it difficult for him to walk.*)

PASCAL. *(sadly)* Bonjour.

QUEEN. Magnificent. They are grotesque!

GAVIN. Thank you. It was only a small matter of surgically implanting pig bladders injected with butter. If your Majesty wishes to feel them…?

QUEEN. Incroyable! They feel absolutely naturale. And what will you do for my lips?

GAVIN. For your lips I have caught a bee, and I will place it in a jar over your mouth and let it sting you. Your lips will swell, and be large and full. The procedure will of course have to be repeated every day.

QUEEN. A small price for beauty. And for my eyes?

GAVIN. For your eyes, I have prepared a tincture made from deadly nightshade, or belladonna, which means "beautiful woman." When dropped into the eyes, this will dilate your pupils to make them dark and beautiful. Though I must warn you, the tincture is also toxic and may produce terrifying hallucinations.

QUEEN. I don't mind that. Let us begin!

FATHER. The French Queen was greatly pleased with the work Gavin did on her, and offered him all the pleasures of her town-palace in gratitude. But not more than a few days would pass when the Queen approached Gavin for new cosmetic procedures. She asked Gavin to give her a tail like a graceful mare, and prosthetic horns, harvested from a reindeer. Though such requests seemed at first eccentric, Gavin assured himself that there were cultural differences to account for. Ideas of beauty were different in France. He did not wish to seem unsophisticated.

(**GAVIN** *appears at a press conference.*)

GAVIN. Yesterday, I strategically implanted fur on her Majesty's back and legs. This morning I will be dying her entire body bright red, the color of blood. For this I'll be using a special dye made from python blood by Egyptian slaves. After lunch, if time permits, I will attempt to make her pet yorkie "less Jewish looking."

FATHER. Gavin became accustomed to life in the town-palace: the wine, the flute players, the dancing girls – Gavin developed quite a taste for the dancing girls. Of course, he never really did anything with them – just titty-fucked them – for his heart still belonged to Amelia. But as days turned to weeks, and months turned to years, Amelia's face in his memory grew dim, and Gavin was hitting the taverns every night until the very wee-est hours.

GAVIN. *(staggering drunkenly in his room)* Fuck you! Don't you know who I am! I'm Gavin-fucking-Nosemaker! I don't have to listen to you, or anybody!

PASCAL. Of course, of course, but if Monsieur would simply allow me to remove his breastplate –

GAVIN. Get your hands off me!!! *(He knocks a bunch of stuff over. His trunk his revealed.)* My trunk! My old trunk! You've hidden it from me.

PASCAL. Of course not Monsieur. Now, if I may inject Monsieur with his special vitamins –

GAVIN. *(hunching proprietarily over his trunk)* Get out!! I said, GET OUT!

(PASCAL leaves and GAVIN begins to open his trunk, removing items.)

My powders and my potions! My bonecracker and my herring knife! And my crucible. The Travel Crucible of Arathorn. How crude these old tools seem now. Oh Wulfric…if you could only see me now.

FATHER. And suddenly he began to nosemake. Gavin didn't know what force guided his hands that night, as he poured out his smelting liquid and wielded his mallet. He did not know what caused visions that began to form behind his eyes, the incantations that sprung from his lips, but it was at once of him and inside of him. He felt the spirits of everyone he had ever known – of Wulfric, and Ulrich, Kent the Gatekeeper, and Jean-Michel too – whispering to him, telling him what to do.

(The people mentioned begin to whisper in his head. We hear lines from earlier in the play. GAVIN begins to work furiously over the crucible.)

WULFRIC. A nosemaker's work is not to improve the work of God, but to mend it when ravaged by the Devil.

KENT. We keep him away from the other boys because we feel like there's something special about him.

ULRICH. Listen to your hands.

JEAN-MICHEL. Whenever you need to pee, pee on something that looks dirty.

WULFRIC. If we tinker too much, we change the nature of the soul.

KENT. Some day he may become a gatekeeper like me.

ULRICH. Listen to your hands.

FATHER. A golden mist arose from the crucible, and finally, from out of the smelting liquid, it emerged. A nose. Scarcely daring to believe it, Gavin reached out and didst take the nose in his hand, examining it, turning it around and around. It was perfect, the most perfect nose Gavin had ever seen. It was warm, soft, made of skin. It was a human nose all right. Gavin had made a human nose.

GAVIN. *(in wonder)* What have I…what have I done?

FATHER. *(shouting)* SUDDENLY, THERE WAS A KNOCK AT THE DOOR! NO! THE DOOR WAS OPENING OF ITS OWN ACCORD! Just in the nick of time, Gavin secreted away the wonderful nose in the pocket of his doublet.

PASCAL. *(entering)* A thousand apologies, Monsieur. Her Majesty requires your presence.

GAVIN. Oh for God's sake…I told her I'm not going to be able to implant her third arm until the human skeletons arrive from Armenia!

PASCAL. I believe this is something else, Monsieur. Now please. We do not wish to anger the Queen.

GAVIN. All right, just let me get dressed.

PASCAL. Her Majesty says that won't be necessary, Monsieur. Come now with me right away.

FATHER. As Gavin followed the manservant, he reflected on how in the dark the night halls of the French Queen's palace, which had begun to seem like home to him, seemed unfamiliar now, almost as if he had never seen them before.

PASCAL. Mind your step, Monsieur. The floor is a bit slippery with human secretions.

FATHER. And then Gavin realized he never *had* seen these halls before, that Pascal was leading him into a part of the palace in which he had never been, almost as if he had never been there. Suddenly, for the first time in a long time, Gavin began to feel afraid.

(Strange wailing music plays.)

GAVIN. Pascal, what is that music?

PASCAL. I hear nothing, Monsieur.

FATHER. Finally, they reached a great stone wall that blocked their path. Gavin raised his hand to strike the manservant for misleading him, when suddenly, he saw in the middle of the wall a small hole, exactly the size, shape and height of one of Gavin's own eyeballs. Fearfully, and with great trepidation – which means the same thing – Gavin looked through the hole! And Oh! What he saw! What he saw!!

GAVIN. Great Zounds! Pascal!

PASCAL. Hmmm?

GAVIN. It's…The Place! The place in France where the naked ladies dance!

PASCAL. Oui, Monsieur. And that is the hole in the wall through which the boys may see it all. The Queen did not wish you to know of the place until the time was ripe. And now, at last, the time, she has fully ripened.

FATHER. *(getting kind of drunk)* Eagerly, Gavin returned his eye to the wondrous hole, anxious to see his fill of the naked ladies. He wanted to stand there forever, watching their undulating buttocks, their bouncing breasts, the fat on their upper arms jiggle in a sexual manner. But suddenly an another eyeball appeared in the hole. Gavin recognized the split yellow pupil he had transplanted from a cryogenically frozen king cobra. It was the Queen of France!

QUEEN. Gavin!!! At last you are here! Come in! Come inside my secret naked chamber!

FATHER. The room was full flaming torches that gave off an eerie red light, and as Gavin's eyes adjusted, he could see that all was not as it should be with the naked ladies. One of them had the legs of a goat, and quite a few of them, Gavin could see, had rather sizeable penises. Did he do that? God he'd been busy lately, he couldn't even remember. A few of the naked ladies were rubbing up against each other in a way Gavin supposed he would have found erotic, had one of them not been a chicken with one enormous boob. The Queen greeted him with a huge hug.

QUEEN. A Toast! There is magnificent news from the Slovakian Forest. Brankavicza the Wonderful is not so wonderful anymore!

GAVIN. You mean?

QUEEN. She is dead! At last, I am the most beautiful woman in the world! Now all I have to do is kill her baby and bathe in its blood, and I will be the most beautiful woman in the world for all eternity! Everybody drink! Drink! Gavin, you're not drinking.

GAVIN. You! You are the Devil!

QUEEN. But of course! And you are the Nosemaker who has at last returned me to my true form! Now Satan shall rule the earth for a thousand years!

GAVIN. No, No!

QUEEN. Yes! Yes! Now you must be rewarded…but wait! Wait! Where are you going! Stop him! STOP HIM!

FATHER. The evil boob chicken pulled a lever, and the wall began to close!! Gavin dived through the opening. The Queen was right behind him – but not fast enough! The wall closed on her, squeezing her body like a vice. Her butter-injected breasts and buttocks bulged pig bladder casings. She made a final angry cry…before exploding like an exploding Chicken Kiev, splattering rancid butter and releasing clouds of newborn flies.

(Sounds of explosions and flies buzzing until **GAVIN** *and* **PASCAL** *are riding horses.)*

PASCAL. Monsieur, can you gallop a little less fast? My boobs are slapping. It is tres painful. Ow! Ow!

GAVIN. Consider that your punishment for almost enabling Satan's thousand-year conquest of the world, Pascal.

PASCAL. Touché.

GAVIN. I'll take you to the bra-monger's when we arrive.

PASCAL. But Monsieur Gavin, where do we go?

GAVIN. Where I belong! To the Nosemaker's Academy of Vienna! For my time with the Queen has soured me completely on private practice, and now I wish to teach. If Ulrich will but take me back!

(sound of explosion)

FATHER. Pascal's breasts exploded. But still the two friends galloped on, until they were far from Paris and its diabolical inhabitants. As they rode through the untamed forest of Central Europe, Gavin could feel his French self completely slipping away. By the time they reached Vienna a week later, he was once again analytical, moody, and anti-Semitic, just like a real Austrian. But in the center of the city, where the Nosemaker's Academy had stood, there was nothing. The school had disappeared, leaving only an empty field. In the middle of the field was a small pile of rubble, on which an old man was seated, his shoulders shaking as he wept.

GAVIN. Old man! What happened here?

*(The man looks up, **GAVIN** sees it is **ULRICH**.)*

Dr. Ulrich! 'Tis you!

ULRICH. Gavin! Oh my boy! That I should live to see this day! *(They embrace.)*

GAVIN. Oh Dr. Ulrich! What have they done to you? And the Academy?

ULRICH. You have not heard? Gavin, all across Europe they are turning against the Nosemakers.

GAVIN. What? Who? Why?

ULRICH. There are many, and from all walks of life: churchmen, nobility, peasants. Europe is full of bitter and deformed people. And they are led by an Englishman from Shropshire. He calls himself Father Percival.

GAVIN. Percival, the faceless knight? He lives?

ULRICH. It was he who has wrought this destruction. He and the other knights of pan-European anti-Nosemaker movement stole into the Academy by cloak of night and burned it to the ground. There were no survivors. Even Rhonda was consigned to the flames. Had I not been at the grocery store at that very moment, I too would have perished in the conflagration.

GAVIN. Ulrich. You are ill. We must get you to a hospital.

ULRICH. There are no hospitals now. You must go Gavin. They will find you here.

GAVIN. But what about you?

ULRICH. My time on this earth is done. I'm dying of old age, and sadness.

GAVIN. No!

ULRICH. Yes…I have only a few more seconds. But wait, I almost forgot. I have something for you. It was salvaged from the fire.

FATHER. From his pocket, the old nosemaker produced a small square of singed paper and handed it to Gavin. Carefully, Gavin unfolded it. The paper was badly charred thickly layered with soot and ashes. There was writing on it, but Gavin could make out only four words: "Dear, Gavin, Love, and Amelia."

GAVIN. Amelia! Amelia! I never did write to her! Oh, Dr. Ulrich. I must return to England. Dr. Ulrich? Dr. Ulrich!

*(**ULRICH** is dead.)*

FATHER. There was no time for a proper burial. Pascal had overheard a prostitute down by the docks say that there was a ship leaving for England in fifteen minutes, and was determined that his master should be on it. In just a few short months, Gavin was gazing 'pon the rocky shores of his beloved England.

GAVIN. Quicken thy step, Pascal, we are almost there!

FATHER. Gavin stopped in his tracks. Before him ruins smoldered. Was all the world ablaze?

*(They notice a **CRAZY BEGGAR** rummaging among the wreckage.)*

GAVIN. You there, beggar, know you what happened to the orphanage that once was here?

BEGGAR. Burned down. For disobeyment. Disobeyment of the law.

GAVIN. What law?

BEGGAR. Father Percival, he's got his laws. So many laws has he.

GAVIN. Then he is returned.

BEGGAR. *(sing-songy)* Burns down he the shops of men, to teach us the discipline. Burns he us to save our souls. Kind kind Father Percival. Oh! But look ye not upon him! Horrible, horrible Father Percival.

GAVIN. I know your face.

BEGGAR. It's a common face.

GAVIN. Kent the Gatekeeper? Kent! It is I, Gavin, your old friend.

BEGGAR. Gavin? Gavin say you? Gavin be no friend of mine. Gavin did not visit me. Gavin left Kent alone with only the crazy boys for company.

GAVIN. Kent –

KENT. Gavin went away with Wulfric. Gavin is Nosemaker now. Nosemakers be forbidden in Percivaltown!

GAVIN. Percivaltown?

KENT. He calls it Percivaltown because Percival is his name and his town it be. He wants to save the souls of his people. But I am insane. I have no soul!

GAVIN. Good god! Wulfric! Amelia!

KENT. SAY NOT GOD'S NAME IN VAIN!! Once did Kent say God's name in vein. Then God sent Father Percival…

GAVIN. No, no!

FATHER. Gavin backed away in horror, then ran. He ran and ran. Finally, he arrived to the place by the English Pines where once stood the house of Wulfric. Like so much else in this shitty world of ours, it was a charred piece of shit.

GAVIN. I'm too late!

(GAVIN *falls to his knees and weeps.* PASCAL *arrives and weeps as well.*)

GAVIN. *(cont.) (weeping)* Master Wulfric and Amelia were the kindest and most beautiful people I've ever known.

PASCAL. Wulfric was the kind one, and Amelia was the beautiful?

GAVIN. Yes. Not that I'd call Wulfric ugly; he had a weak chin maybe, but generally regular features, if only he took care of himself better… but Amelia! – Amelia was kind *and* beautiful! She was my one true love. Oh God, how could you let such a fate befall a man and woman so kind and beautiful, respectively?! Why should you hurl such anger upon the nosemakers of the world?! Do you smite us for our arrogance, that we might perfect the bodies of your children? Or are you just a spiteful dick?

PASCAL. Gavin, that is God you are speaking to…

GAVIN. And what of it? All my life I have spent trying to make people beautiful, to bring honor to God's creations, to perfect those he hath hurled into this world half-formed or broken. For not one day have I lived without thinking of how I may best serve and honor him…

PASCAL. Except for the years in France.

GAVIN. Except for the years in France, when I lost my way. But it was God who put France before me, and God who created this sick and evil world. This is His design. I shall deign to improve it no more. *(GAVIN lifts up his satchel and dumps his instruments on the ground.)*

PASCAL. No, Master! You are the only nosemaker in Europe now ! You must carry on the tradition and pass it down.

GAVIN. To who? I saved myself for marriage all these years, never had real intercourse because I wanted to save myself for the woman I loved. And now she's dead. If anyone wants me, I'll be at the whorehouse. If it's still there.

FATHER. It was. There was a limit to even Father Percival's religious mania. But long gone were the local beauties Gavin remembered. The whores of Percivaltown looked like plague victims. Grimacing, Gavin smeared his body with antiseptic gel and waited at the bar for his number to come up.

GAVIN. *(drunkenly)* Beauty is a child's game. Only temporary fixes. Nothing lasts. You want to know what perfection is? Close your eyes. That's perfection. Everything else is rot.

(He covers his face. **AMELIA**, *now a hideously syphilitic whore without a face, appears behind him. She is missing her nose.)*

AMELIA. Do not confuse God's perfection for your own. What seems to you so wrong is all just part of his plan.

GAVIN. I've heard those words before…and in that voice… Amelia! Can it be?

AMELIA. Amelia, says he. Aye, there was an Amelia once, but she be dead. They call me Brandi now. Brandi the Whore.

GAVIN. Sweet Amelia! Do you not know me? 'Tis I! 'Tis Gavin!

AMELIA. Gavin! Gavin, how can it be?

FATHER. And at once, a scarlet blush arose on the pock-marked cheeks of the ruined girl, and she wiped the garish rouge from what was left of her lips and put both her breasts back inside her blouse, for she was ashamed.

AMELIA. Gavin, I am ashamed. I fear you find me muchly changed.

GAVIN. Oh Amelia, once fair Amelia – what has happened to you?

AMELIA. I wrote you. Every day for seven years. Didn't you get my letters?

GAVIN. I…well, I was travelling around a lot.

AMELIA. It doesn't matter. I am sorry to say that my looks are the least of the changes wrought on the village of Ogilvy-on-Mather.

GAVIN. Amelia, what was become of your father?

(Her eyes clouded with emotion, she cannot speak all at once.)

AMELIA. They came for Wulfric by night. They bound him, blinded him, shorn him of his beard, and dragged him off to the dungeon of Percival, to await execution. I walked through the night to the castle and begged him to spare my father's life. He refused. I offered him my body. He accepted.

GAVIN. Amelia, no!

AMELIA. But even as my violation was completed, mine own dear father's body was being licked by the fire! I was deceived! And it was not just Wulfric the Nosemaker burnt that day, but Iolanthe the Wigmaker and Cadogan the Finger Repairman. Even Brian the Makeup Artist was consigned to the flames. For Percival is the enemy of Beauty. He is the enemy of grace. He is the enemy of God!

GAVIN. Oh Amelia! How I wish you weren't ruined, so that I could marry you…

AMELIA. But I *am* ruined now, Gavin, marked forever with my sin. Not even my father would help me now. If only thou hadst married me these fourteen years ago, as thou didst solemnly promise that thy wouldst! Or at least broken off the engagement so I could have moved on with my life! But 'tis no matter now. I am beyond salvation, until I be redeemed to Hell.

GAVIN. Amelia, believe me, I thought always of you! But I had to go away, to help people.

AMELIA. And who have you helped? Who? In all your travels, with all your skills, have you made one broken person whole again?

HARALD FLEETFOOT. *(as* **WAITER**, *entering)* Excuse me. That'll be six seventy-five please.

FATHER. Gavin reached into the pocket of his doublet to draw out the coins. But instead of the familiar chill of silver, he felt something else. Something warm. Something soft. Something…human.

(It is the nose. The human nose.)

AMELIA. Gavin, what is that in your hand?

GAVIN. Amelia. Dear Amelia! *(He embraces her tightly.)*

AMELIA. Ow! I have osteoperosis!

GAVIN. Darling Amelia! For over 13 years I have studied and wandered the earth, dedicating myself to the art and science of nosemaking. I have gazed upon the most beautiful women of France and one woman in Austria, and pictures in books of women in other places. I have gazed upon and admired their shoulders and their breasts and their buttocks, but most of all I have contemplated their noses. And the sum of my efforts, and all my years of study is this: the nose of the first woman I ever laid eyes on. It is your nose, Amelia, and I realize now that I have but journeyed all these years only so that I mayst return it to thee.

AMELIA. Oh Gavin. And with this nose, you give me back my soul.

FATHER. And with that, Gavin placed the nose to her face, filling the gaping maw and sealing itself in place. And it was as if her whole body were restored at once, for the power which flowed through the nose was not only that of science, but of God, and magic, and love. But before Gavin and Amelia could steal away to the bathroom to consummate the love they had held inside them all these years…

(Sound FX of Percival, whooshing, etc.)

FATHER PERCIVAL. BRAAAAAA!!!

AMELIA. No! Please, Father Percival, not the stake! He has done nothing to you, and see how he has restored my face. My face is beautiful again. If you like, you may put your penis in it. But let my fiancé live!

FATHER PERCIVAL. BRAAAH! BRAAA, BRAAA, BRAAAA, BRAAAAAAH

GAVIN. No, Father Percival *you* are wrong! Letting the flames remove our wicked flesh will not restore us in spirit. For the spirit of the soul and flesh cannot be divided. And just as one must cultivate the soul, so must one care for the body. And perhaps if you would only let me operate on you, I might restore some of that happiness which you have lost…

FATHER PERCIVAL. BRAAAAAAHH!!

GAVIN. As you wish. Only spare my sweet Amelia.

FATHER PERCIVAL. BRAAAAAAAAAA!!!

GAVIN. No, not Amelia, too!

FATHER. And so Amelia and Gavin were carried from the place, and lashed to a single stake, and the faggots were lain below them. Quickly a crowd was formed, larger than usual because it was Friday night, but also because Gavin's name was known throughout the land. In the crowd Gavin could see the faces of those he had worked on as a boy. There was Sally with the Cleft Lip and Jurgen with the Cauliflower Ears. Even Mistress Purdy, who once flirted with Gavin every chance she had, now called for his excruciating death, loudly as all the others. Could they truly hate him so much? Gavin wondered what would have become of him if Wulfric had chosen another boy that night in the Ivanhoe Home. He might have died of typhus or the plague. He might have become a drug dealer or even a hustler, turning tricks on the King's Highway in exchange for little pieces of cheese or sausage. He wondered if that would have made him happy. Perhaps it would have. But this was no time for regrets, for the faggots had been lighted, and Gavin must bid adieu to life.

AMELIA. I will always love you, Gavin.

GAVIN. And I you, Amelia.

FATHER. And then the flames rose up, and burned off the flesh from their bones, and their souls went to heaven. And Father Percival kept the fires stoked for 3 days, so that even the bones of Gavin and Amelia were reduced to ashes. But of them one thing remained: the nose. Though it was scorched by flame, its flesh would not burn, for it was the Flesh of God. And though Europe reverted to cosmetic and reconstructive barbarism, the legend of Gavin the Nosemaker lived on, inspiring generations of rogue healers like myself, and the Brotherhood of Underground Surgeons, that I am starting tomorrow...after I get some sleep.

(**FATHER** *by this point is very drunk, and his daughter very disturbed by his story.*)

LITTLE GIRL. Oh Daddy, that was a horrible story.

FATHER. Yes, it was. And now you understand why I must do my goodly work in secret.

LITTLE GIRL. But Daddy, what happens if they catch you, doing your secret goodly work? Will they burn us at the stake too?

FATHER. Maybe, depends what country we're in...

LITTLE GIRL. *(softly, exasperated)* America.

FATHER. Then probably they'll just put me in jail. But someone else will rise to take my place. For as long as there is mutilation and deformity and fat people and flat-chested people and old people, there shall be nosemakers, to restore and beautify the body of man.

LITTLE GIRL. But isn't it pointless? If we all end up dead in the end?

FATHER. Nothing is pointless. Not if we bring some beauty to the world. We have our setbacks, like syphilis, and divorce and even death, but it's all worth if we end up like Gavin the Nosemaker – who made a magic nose of real human flesh.

LITTLE GIRL. *(overtired)* Daddy, I'm in third grade now. I'm too old for these kind of stories.

FATHER. You don't believe me?

LITTLE GIRL. No. There's no such thing as magic noses. Only death. Now please just go away. I have to go to sleep. I have a spelling test tomorrow.

FATHER. Okay, sweetie. You're right. It was all just a story. Just a story. Goodnight.

(He tucks her in. She turns on her side, and quickly falls asleep, but **FATHER** *lingers in the room. He opens a box, from which he removes the real human nose of Gavin the Nosemaker, which he holds up to the light. It fills him with wonder. Blackout).*

The End

OTHER TITLES AVAILABLE FROM SAMUEL FRENCH

ADRIFT IN MACAO

Book and Lyrics by Christopher Durang
Music by Peter Melnick

Musical / 4m, 3f / Unit Sets

Nominated for a Drama Desk Award for Best Music

Set in 1952 in Macao, China, *Adrift in Macao* is a loving parody of film noir movies. Everyone that comes to Macao is waiting for something, and though none of them know exactly what that is, they hang around to find out. The characters include your film noir standards, like Laureena, the curvaceous blonde, who luckily bumps into Rick Shaw, the cynical surf and turf casino owner her first night in town. She ends up getting a job singing in his night club – perhaps for no reason other than the fact that she looks great in a slinky dress. And don't forget about Mitch, the American who has just been framed for murder by the mysterious villain McGuffin. With songs and quips, puns and farcical shenanigans, this musical parody is bound to please audiences of all ages.

"And there are of course those songs…Melnick demonstrates an affinity for melody and old-fashioned showmanship that link him to his grandfather, Richard Rodgers…"
– Matthew Murray, *Talkin' Broadway*

"With a drop-dead funny book and shamefully silly lyrics by Christopher Durang and lethally catchy music by Peter Melnick. *Adrift In Macao* lovingly parodies the Hollywood film noir classics of the 1940's and 50's…"
– Michael Dale, *BroadwayWorld*

www.ingramcontent.com/pod-product-compliance
Lightning Source LLC
Chambersburg PA
CBHW070418120726
47909CB00005B/1694